Shelby Shoes

by *Sue Ellen Miner*
Sue Ellen Miner 🐾

illustrated by
Tracey Arvidson 🐾

Dedicated to Shelby, my beloved 12 year old Golden Retriever, who was my soul mate with a most golden heart of gold.

Shelby
~loved unconditionally, making us hope we could one day be the humans she already believed us to be
~shared unselfishly, even greeting strangers at the door with a toy
~was beautiful inside and out, especially with her crooked smile
~exuded confidence, elegantly and with humility
~was an amazing big sister to Abby
~loved to please, loved to please, loved to please
~was loyal, defining the word loyalty
~smiled often, with a sweet squint of her soft eyes
~shared love with everyone she met
~retrieved our newspaper, including the larger Sunday edition
~had a cute waddle
~was extremely obedient
~was perfect!

Shelby, may your memory live on and may you, once again, find your way into the hearts of others and make them smile.

Also dedicated to my closest family members who believed in me when I told them I would one day write *Shelby Shoes*—Phil, Brady, Jelena, Davor, Nick, Andrea, Mallory, Scott, Hidee, PawPaw, Gran and Popeye. Thank you for being my greatest fans, my best supporters and my favorite listeners.

This is Shelby Shoes.

Shelby Shoes shakes.

Shelby Shoes shares, and...

Shelby Shoe's Toys

Shelby Shoes surely likes
being someone's shadow.

But... does Shelby Shoes
really wear shoes?

NO!

Shelby Shoes does not wear shoes.
That would surely be so silly.

Shelby Shoes is Shelby Shoes,

because...

Giggles Girdle is Giggles Girdle,

and...

Peaches Pajamas is Peaches Pajamas,

and...

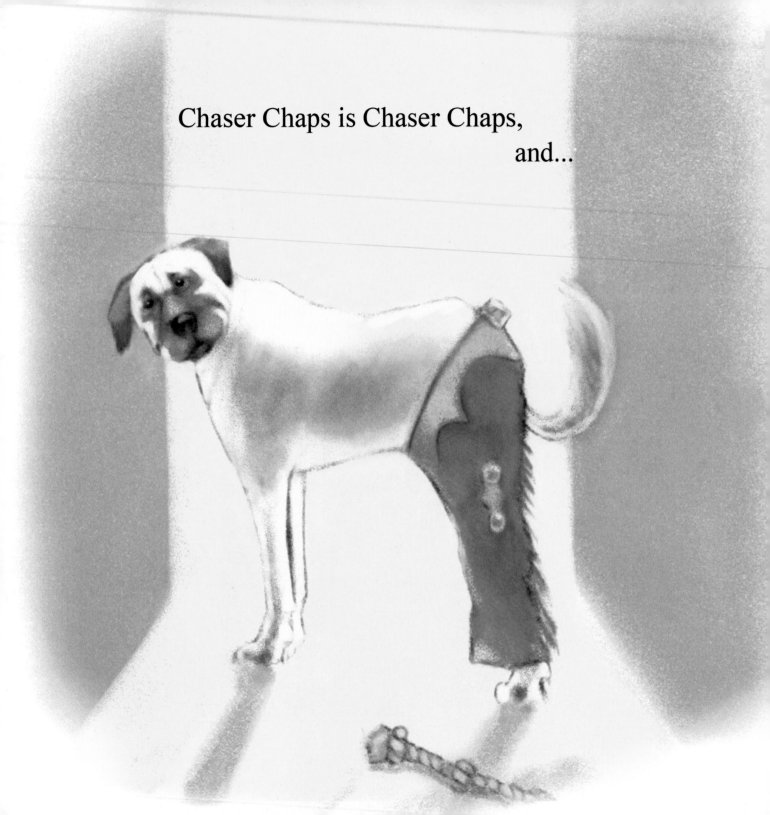

Chaser Chaps is Chaser Chaps,

and...

Flossie Flip Flops is Flossie Flip Flops, and...

Ziggy Zipper is Ziggy Zipper.

WHAT?

Shelby Shoes,

Giggles Girdle,

Peaches Pajamas,

Chaser Chaps,

Flossie Flip Flops,

and Ziggy Zipper?

Does Giggles Girdle wear a girdle?

NO!

Giggles Girdle does not wear a girdle.
That would surely be so silly.

Does Peaches Pajamas wear pajamas?

NO!

Peaches Pajamas does not wear pajamas.
That would surely be so silly.

Does Chaser Chaps wear chaps?

NO!

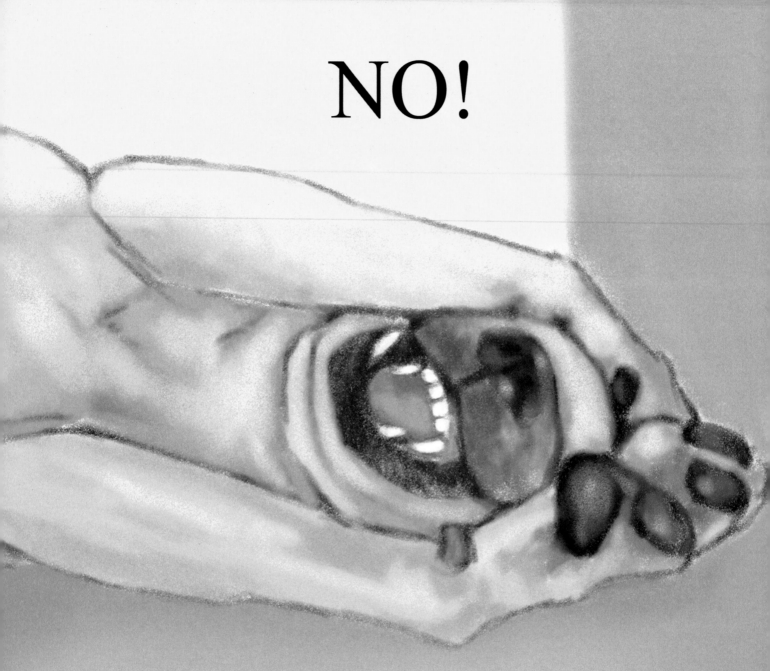

Chaser Chaps does not wear chaps.
That would surely be so silly.

Does Flossie Flip Flops wear flip flops?

NO!

Flossie Flip Flops does not wear flip flops.
That would surely be so silly.

Does Ziggy Zipper wear a zipper?

NO! NO!

NO!

Ziggy Zipper does not wear a zipper!
That would surely be so silly.

Shelby Shoes is Shelby Shoes, because…

Shelby Shoes has a name that surely sounds so silly, and...

that makes us smile.

Shhhhhhhhhhhh...

Shelby Shoes sure is sheepy...

I mean sleepy.